The Great Zoo-Baloo!

Written and Illustrated by Sarah Davison

DEDICATION

For everyone everywhere who cares about wildlife protection and preservation.

"A Zoo-Baloo? What is a Zoo-Baloo?" you may ask.

"It's when a hullabaloo happens in a zoo," I reply.

"But what is a hullabaloo?" you may ask again.

"Well, imagine that all the animals in the zoo have the chance to do whatever they want to do, go wherever they want to go, and there is no-one about to stop them. Imagine it getting louder and louder and more and more out of control…that is a hullabaloo in a zoo.

Or, as the animals came to call this one,

'The Great Zoo-Baloo!' "

The Great Zoo-Baloo!

Angus is asked to look after the zoo all by himself.

"Me?" said Angus in amazement? "You want ME to look after the whole zoo and all of the animals on my OWN?"

Everybody in the meeting turned and looked at the youngest zoo keeper. This was his first day working at the zoo and he was so little that his uniform didn't even fit him properly.

"Yes, Angus," said the Big Boss decisively. "There's nothing else for it. We have to save money while the zoo is shut. Will you do it?"

Angus gulped and went a little bit red. "Yes," he said in a very quiet, not so sure voice.

And so began The Great Zoo-Baloo!

To begin with, everything seemed to run smoothly. Angus fed the animals and cleaned and cared for the zoo and, though the animals thought it was a bit quiet, most didn't really notice any difference.

But one did. Peanuts the parrot, a blue and yellow macaw, was a particularly clever and nosy bird. He enjoyed watching the visitors and keepers that normally passed his cage and he soon began to realize that, apart from Angus, there was nobody else about.

His clever bird brain began working. If nobody was about, then surely that meant he could have a little bit of fun? In fact, couldn't all the animals have a little bit of fun? They had all spent a lot of time watching the visitors and seeing them enjoy themselves, and it had given them each ideas of things they too would like to try.

So that evening, when Angus came round to feed the parrots their tea, Peanuts had a plan. He waited till Angus bent over to pick up the feeding pail and, quick as lightning, he stuck his head through the bars and, ever so gently, pulled the set of keys to the zoo from Angus' pocket and hid them under his wing.

Naughty Peanuts the parrot pinches the keys to the zoo.

Angus did not feel a thing. He just carried on walking out of the zoo with his pail and let the gate lock shut behind him.

Peanuts was delighted! He bobbed up and down on his branch doing a little dance, holding the keys in his beak! "I'm such a clever macaw!" he thought to himself. "Now for the next part of my plan!"

Peanuts waited till he saw Angus bike away home for his tea, then he knew it was perfectly safe to put the rest of his plan in action. He carefully held the keys in his claws and unlocked the padlock to his cage. He had watched the keepers do this so many times, and he had been practicing with bits of twigs he found at the bottom of his aviary – and in no time at all he was free!

Wasting no time, Peanuts made his way round every cage in the zoo, unlocking each and every one of them, then he flew into the middle of the zoo and let out a loud "SQUARK!! Come and see! Look at me! I'm so clever, I've set you free!" he sang loudly.

At first the animals were a bit confused. Most of them had been enjoying the quieter days to catch up on sleep, so they were surprised to hear Peanuts' song. One by one, they discovered their cage doors were open and they carefully made their way out to the middle of the zoo where Peanuts was waiting for them, looking very proud of himself.

"I've let you all out!" he said boastfully. "I'm such a clever macaw! Now you can explore the whole zoo! No more cages!"

No more cages? The animals began to feel excited. This could be really fun! There were flamingos, vultures, love birds, spider monkeys, howler monkeys, lemurs, maned wolves, snow leopards and sea lions to name just a few, all standing in the middle of the zoo thinking about Peanut's startling news. Every animal, big or small, was present…well, every animal except one…

Peanuts unlocks all of the cages!

"Ummm…" said an important voice. "Excuse me!"

Everyone turned to see who was speaking. At the back of the crowd, looking rather severe, was Sam, the American Bald Eagle.

"It might have escaped your notice," Sam said slowly, "but the cages also keep us safe."

"Yes, I know that," said Peanuts blithely, "but we are all friends here, it's not like any of us would eat each other, is it?!" Peanuts began to laugh - but the others didn't.

"What about Tiger?" asked Sam.

Tiger? TIGER! Peanuts had not thought about the tiger and now all the animals were looking at him accusingly! Where even was the tiger? How could he have been so stupid? The tiger was the most dangerous animal in the zoo and everyone knew it! Now the animals were not looking at him with happy faces at all!

Peanuts thought quickly. "Has anybody seen the tiger?" he asked.

"He was still asleep on his tree house platform when I came past," said one little monkey.

"So, you could lock him back in again," suggested Sam, "and then we can all go back to our cages to safety."

Peanuts looked embarrassed. "I can't," he mumbled.

"Pardon?" said Sam. "Speak up!"

"I said I can't," repeated Peanuts. "You see, I've only ever practiced unlocking cages, not locking them back up again."

OH NO! The tiger can get out!
Phew, he is asleep.
Don't wake the tiger!

"Well, we shall just have to go back to our cages and barricade ourselves in…" began Sam, but he was interrupted by the other animals.

"Oh no, I want to explore!" said the little monkey.

"Me too!" said another.

"And me!" lots more animals said. (You see, the chance to explore the zoo comes along so rarely that the animals really wanted to make the most of it and they weren't going to listen to sensible Sam.)

"We should be alright," said Peanuts slowly, "as long as we don't wake the tiger."

"Yes!" said all the animals at once. "Of course! We must remember, 'Don't Wake the Tiger!'"

Sam gave a very big sigh and headed back to his cage to wait for disaster to happen.

The first to make the most of her freedom was the beautiful snow leopard. It had been a particularly hot season and she had been interested to see the visitors that peered into her cage eating something that looked cool and refreshing. She had noticed that they appeared to come from a building not far from her enclosure, so off she went to explore.

It was the restaurant and inside, to her great excitement, she found the ice-cream freezer. Lifting the lid, she climbed inside and stretched out, enjoying the feeling of the frozen ice-creams cooling her body.

 "Ahhh," she said to herself, "so this must be what snow feels like!" and she dozed off comfortably, the coolest she had ever felt.

The animals explore the zoo.
The snow leopard cools off in the ice-cream freezer.

Next to make the most of their opportunity were the maned wolves. Now, to let you into a little secret, and one that is not really a secret if you have ever been to the zoo and seen these creatures, it has to be said that these animals are incredibly smelly. I mean, they *really* pong. What you won't know is that they are actually rather embarrassed by this. Every time a visitor walks past holding their nose and making some rude comment about body odour, the maned wolves are quite offended. Now was their chance to change this! Grabbing their shower gels and shampoos they dashed to the waterfall in the sea lion's enclosure and had the best bubbly shower of their lives!

The sea lions were not impressed. Not in the slightest! They began to complain loudly.

"Shh!" said the maned wolves. "Don't wake the tiger!"

The maned wolves take a shower.

Next to have fun were the lemurs. These inquisitive animals had soon found the adventure playground and the baby lemurs were playing in the sand and riding the roundabout, just a bit too fast, giggling happily.

The baby lemurs enjoy the playground.

The teenage lemurs, however, were agilely climbing all over the high wire assault course, jumping and bounding about and daring each other to jump further and higher. They began making quite a lot of noise, as teenagers often do.

The teenage lemurs get noisy as they climb.

"Shh!" hissed several animals at once. "Don't wake the tiger!"

But the tiger was asleep.

Meanwhile, over the other side of the zoo, the otters had put a long held dream into action. They loved eating fish, and from their enclosure, for years, they could see a large fish pond. This had been so tempting for them… and so they decided to move there. In no time they had settled in and were enjoying a rest by the pond edge, dreaming of their next meal.

The otters move house to the fish pond.

The fish were not so happy and blew bubbles in annoyance.

"Don't wake the tiger!" the otters told them rather cheekily.

By the Australian paddock, the red kangaroo had found an interesting use for her pouch. With careful jiggling, she had managed to unlock the nearby vending machine and now her pouch was full of chocolate, sweets and crisps and she was making a little money hopping round, selling them to an eager queue of hungry animal customers.

"Don't wake the tiger!" she said to them as they munched happily.

The kangaroo sells sweets from her pouch.

Perhaps the animal having the most unusual experience of his life was the sloth. Now, as you may know, the sloth is an incredibly slow animal and it takes a very long time to get anywhere. So, to speed the sloth up a bit, two monkeys had "borrowed" a zorbing ball from the adventure playground, tipped the sloth inside and were happily bowling him around the zoo so he could see everything. Round and round he went, whizzing past the animal cages and all around the zoo, getting dizzier and dizzier and faster and faster until finally he crashed into the Farm Barn.

"SHH!" said lots of animals at once. "Don't wake the tiger!"

But the tiger was still asleep…

The slow sloth takes a fast ride around the zoo.

Is the tiger still asleep?

And by now The Great Zoo-Baloo was in full swing. The animals were having an amazing time and things were really beginning to get out of hand. Milo, the hairy armadillo, believed himself to be the fastest creature on four legs in the zoo and had been having timed races with the cheetahs. Eventually, when he realised he wasn't all that fast in comparison, he decided to borrow a remote control car from the souvenir shop and see if he could beat them while riding on it. A crowd had now gathered and was cheering him on.

Milo the armadillo gets some help to race the cheetah.

Also having visited the souvenir shop, the giraffes were making everyone laugh out loud as they had decided to try and disguise themselves with some clothing, saying they were getting fed up of being so easily noticed and standing out so clearly wherever they were.

The giraffes try a disguise

Not surprisingly, the monkeys had been busy making mischief and having the time of their lives. Some of them had also explored the souvenir shop. Beginning with the sweet stand they had tasted every variety on sale - though the bubblegum rather surprised them!

The monkeys taste the sweets.

Next they had a wonderful time playing hide and seek amongst all the toys on the shelves…

…and the toys in the baskets…

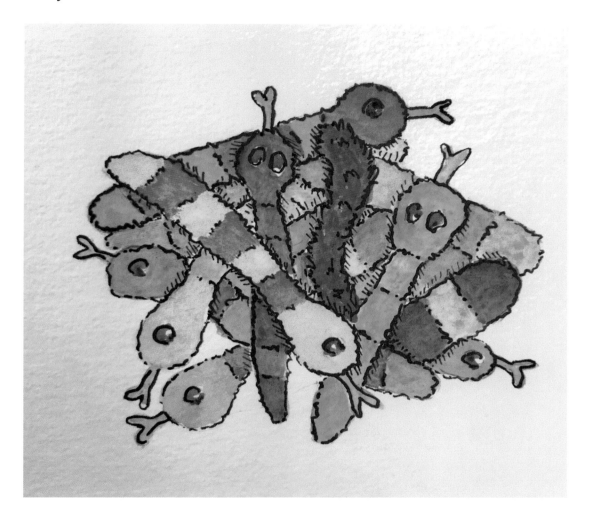

The monkeys hide in the shop.

Worse though, two had even managed to get into the reception office and onto the computer.

The monkeys go on the computer.

Meanwhile, back outside, several other creatures had also decided to disguise themselves. The red panda, fed up with hearing visitors saying "That's not a panda, it's not black and white" every time they saw him, raided the zoo store and found some black and white paints. He was sitting having a lovely time painting himself the colours of a Giant Panda.

The zebras too had got in on the act and had decided to become normal horses so had disguised themselves black or white. Then they picked on the smallest zebra and painted him in checks!

The animals paint themselves black and white.

Once the monkeys saw the black and white paint that the red panda and zebras were using, they happily rolled in it and made as many paw prints along the paths as they could. As the paint started to dry and their fur began to go stiff, they decided to take a bath in the basin in the toilets. There they had great fun playing with all of the toilet rolls and soap and splashing water everywhere.

The monkeys make a mess.

The animals were getting louder and louder. Sam was getting more and more worried. He kept trying to say "Don't wake the tiger!" but by now no-one was listening! In despair, Sam packed his back pack and headed back to America (on foot as he did not like flying after an unfortunate incident when he was mobbed by birds during a flying display).

Sam the Eagle is fed up with the noise and leaves the zoo.

Finally, at the other side of the zoo, the marmots had been having the time of their lives. These little creatures love burrowing and making underground tunnels, so, as soon as they has been let loose, had decided to put their Grand Plan into action that would link up every cage with an underground tunnel. They got so carried away that they forgot to check what was above them and they burrowed right underneath the Snack Shack making a bigger and bigger hole! The Snack Shack began to wobble, then tremble, then shake as its foundations were removed until finally it fell into the hole with a deafening

CRASH!

The Snack Shack falls with a big "CRASH!"

Every animal froze.

They held their breath.

Then…

ROAR!!!!!

The tiger is AWAKE!

"Who's been making this hullabaloo in the zoo?!" the tiger roared.

Slowly Peanuts came forward, and trembling rather violently, he told the tiger how he had opened all of the cages. Then, one by one, the animals came forward and explained what they had been doing while no human being was around.

The tiger looked thoughtful. The animals waited for him to punish them, but instead a twinkle came into his eye.

"I see," the tiger said slowly. "So really, you were just making the most of an opportunity?"

The animals nodded.

"You have made a terrible mess, however. Each of you needs to clean up the mess you have made, then report back to me as soon as you have finished.

The animals nodded and scurried off to put things right.

Some time later everything was spick and span at the zoo. The ice-creams were back in the freezer, the zorbing ball was back by the playground, the paint was all washed away, the clothing returned and the toilets cleaned. Apart from a clean, soapy smell by the maned wolves' area, and one toy car left by the armadillo cage, everything was back to normal.

The animals returned to the tiger.

"Well done," he said. "You have put everything right and now I have arranged a treat."

And out from behind his platform the tiger drove the zoo train! He drove them round and round the zoo until it was nearly time for Angus to start work the next morning, then he locked the train up in its garage and every animal went back to their cage and went fast asleep.

It was the greatest Zoo-Baloo ever!

The animals tidy up then enjoy lots of rides on the zoo train as a reward.

When Angus turned up for work the next morning, he had to use his spare key to get into the zoo as he couldn't find his set of keys anywhere. He was pleased to see how tidy everywhere looked, but got a bit of a shock when he found all of the cage doors unlocked! Fortunately, and with much relief, he spotted his set of zoo keys by Peanut's cage.

 "I must have dropped them there last night!" he thought to himself. He quickly went around and locked up all of the cages. "I can't think how I left all of the doors unlocked!" he thought. "Good job nobody knows. I don't think I will tell anyone!"

But we know, don't we?

Other books by Sarah Davison

Something Scary!

And Hide and Seek

By Sarah Davison

"But WHY can't we go to toddlers?"

Written for young children during lockdown in 2020, Harvey Mouse explores what is happening and also plays his favourite game.

Bored, Bored, Bored!

And So Sorry

By Sarah Davison

"I'm bored!" he said. "Bored, bored, bored!"
The second book in the series. Harvey Mouse has been so busy he has run out of things to do! He also makes a messy mistake.

And coming next: "TROLL!"*

"I'm going to be a Truly Terrifying Troll!" Troll said crossly. "No more being sad that nobody likes me!"
Troll scares everyone until he meets one brave little girl who refuses to be frightened…but why?

*working title

About the Author

Sarah has spent most of her life working with children, is married and has 3 teenage daughters of her own. She has been writing and illustrating stories since she was a child, but only began to publish them in spring 2020 when searching for a way to communicate to the children in the pre-school group that she leads. The time spent at home during the Covid 19 Pandemic proved to be the springboard to fulfilling a long held dream.

Inspiration for "The Great Zoo – Baloo!" also came from lockdown. When the zoos closed, Sarah imagined what might happen if no humans were about and the animals could show their true characters while running free. Having spent lots of time at her local zoo when her children were young, she had plenty of animal characters to draw from.

"I think it is so important to support our zoos, especially at this time. They are such an important resource in the protection and preservation of wildlife. I hope that this story will encourage more support for them and the animals that they care for."

January 2021

<u>Keep in touch with Sarah's new releases!</u>
 Follow Sarah on Amazon by searching "Sarah Elizabeth Davison" and clicking "follow".
On Instagram: sarahedavison
On Facebook: on the public "Sarah Davison- Author" page.
Or to be added to her mailing list please email sarahdavisonauthor@gmail.com to receive updates about future events and book releases.

Printed in Great Britain
by Amazon